Albert's Christmas

Special thanks to some special helpers—
Gene Haury, Hugh Kiely, and,
as always, Con Pederson

Atheneum Books for Young Readers
An imprint of Simon & Schuster Children's Publishing Division
1230 Avenue of the Americas
New York, New York 10020

Book design by Angela Carlino
The text of this book is set in Wilke Bold.
The illustrations are rendered in gouache.

First Edition

Printed in the United States of America
10 9 8 7 6 5 4 3 2 1

Library of Congress Cataloging-in-Publication Data
Tryon, Leslie.
Albert's Christmas / by Leslie Tryon.—1st ed.
p.   cm.
Summary: Albert the duck and his friends help Santa
as he races on his annual visit.
ISBN 0-689-81034-2
[1. Ducks—Fiction. 2. Animals—Fiction. 3. Santa Claus—Fiction.
4. Christmas—Fiction. 5. Stories in rhyme.] I. Title.
PZ7.T7865Alh   1997
[E]—dc20
96-25762

Albert's Christmas

written & illustrated by **Leslie Tryon**

ATHENEUM BOOKS FOR YOUNG READERS

For Jon Lanman

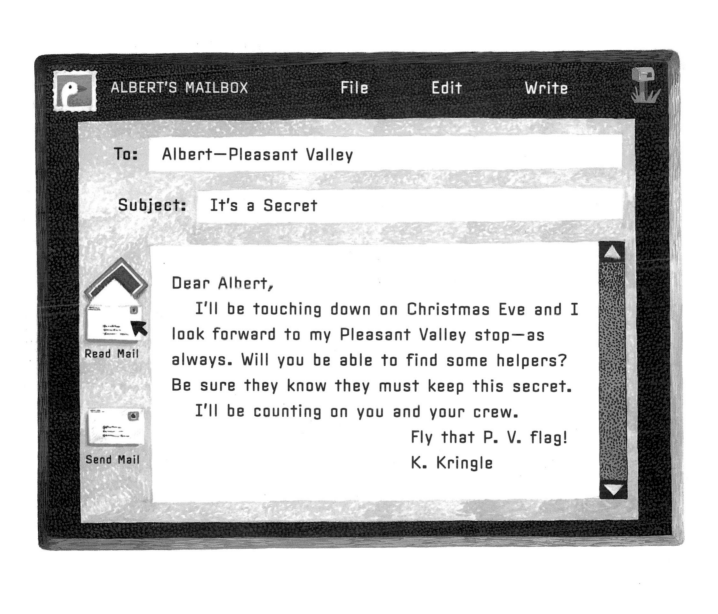

Ever so quietly, rise from your sleep.
Don't make a sound, not even a peep.

Your ride is waiting. I know the way.
The moon is as bright as Christmas Day.

There's work to be done. We've got to hurry.
So hang on tight, and please don't worry.

He'll circle in low. Just look for the light.
Red and green twinkling stars in the night.

Sing Kringle O, Jingle O, Jolly Ho Ho!
I've got a secret that you will soon know.

Up in the hills there's a place we will go
To help with his landing by shouting out . . .

A blizzard kicks up as they *scree-eee-ch* into place,
At the very first pit stop in Santa's big race.

Welcome dear Santa! On behalf of the crew,
We offer this gift, made especially for you.

If you're ready, helpers, I'll start the clock.
Twelve minutes and counting! *Tick-tock, tick-tock.*

First get the reindeer their bags of gruel,
And jack up the sleigh while they refuel.

Tip-toe across their sleek harnessed backs,
Then rub their antlers with flying wax.

Scrape the runners. Position the block.
Ten minutes to go! *Tick-tock, tick-tock.*

Comb through his eyebrows, his beard, and his hair.
That sleeve is in need of a little repair.

His tummy is grumbling.
It's time for a snack.
He needs extra strength
to lift that huge sack.

His lunch pail is empty.
Be sure to restock.
Just eight minutes left.
Tick-tock, tick-tock.

Quick! Buff the bell, his boots, and his buckle
While I tickle his belly to check out his chuckle.

Squeegee the windshield. Make it all clear.
He must see every last chimney down here.

With all of this stardust there's really no way
He could ever see past the hood of his sleigh.

Now lower the jack. Pull out the block.
Six minutes to go. *Tick-tock, tick-tock.*

Thirty-two hooves! Let's see some action.
File 'em rough to create better traction.

Study the starmap with all the reindeer,
And then with their gift-giving charioteer.

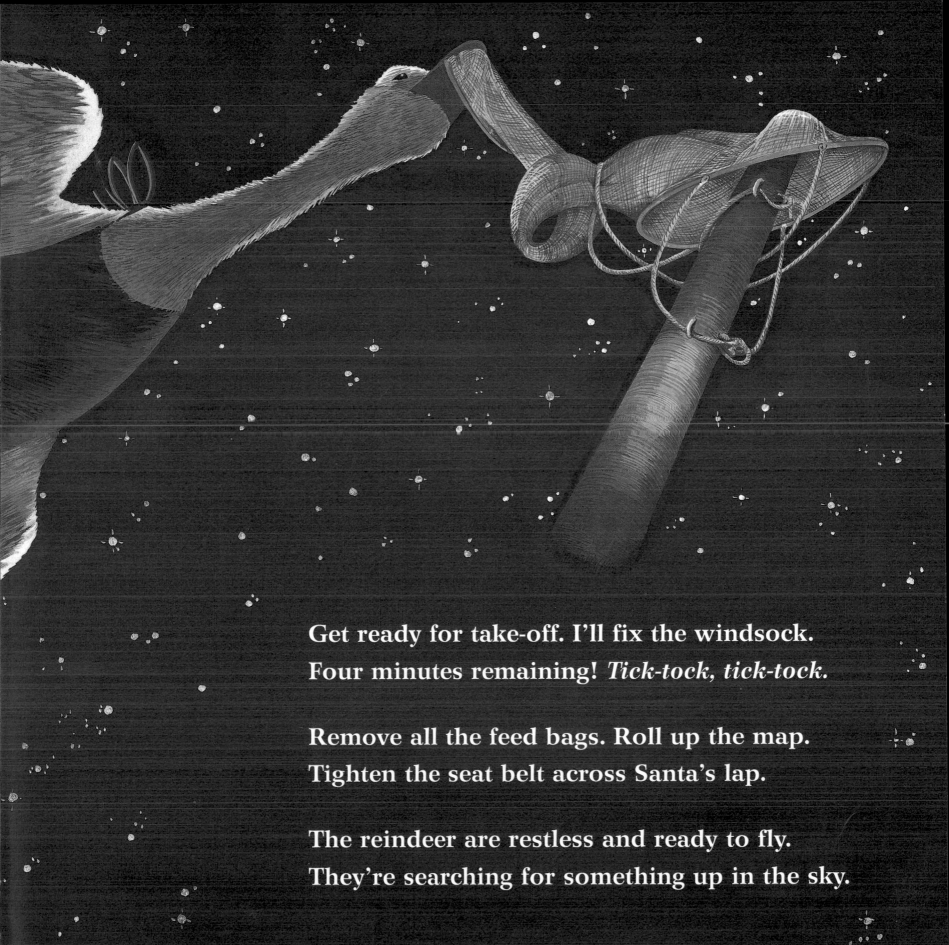

Get ready for take-off. I'll fix the windsock.
Four minutes remaining! *Tick-tock, tick-tock.*

Remove all the feed bags. Roll up the map.
Tighten the seat belt across Santa's lap.

The reindeer are restless and ready to fly.
They're searching for something up in the sky.

Toss Santa his cap. Watch out! Clear the dock!
Two minutes to liftoff. *Tick-tock, tick-tock.*

We're down to five seconds. All systems are go:
Five . . . four . . . three,
two . . . one,
and *ZEE-RO!*

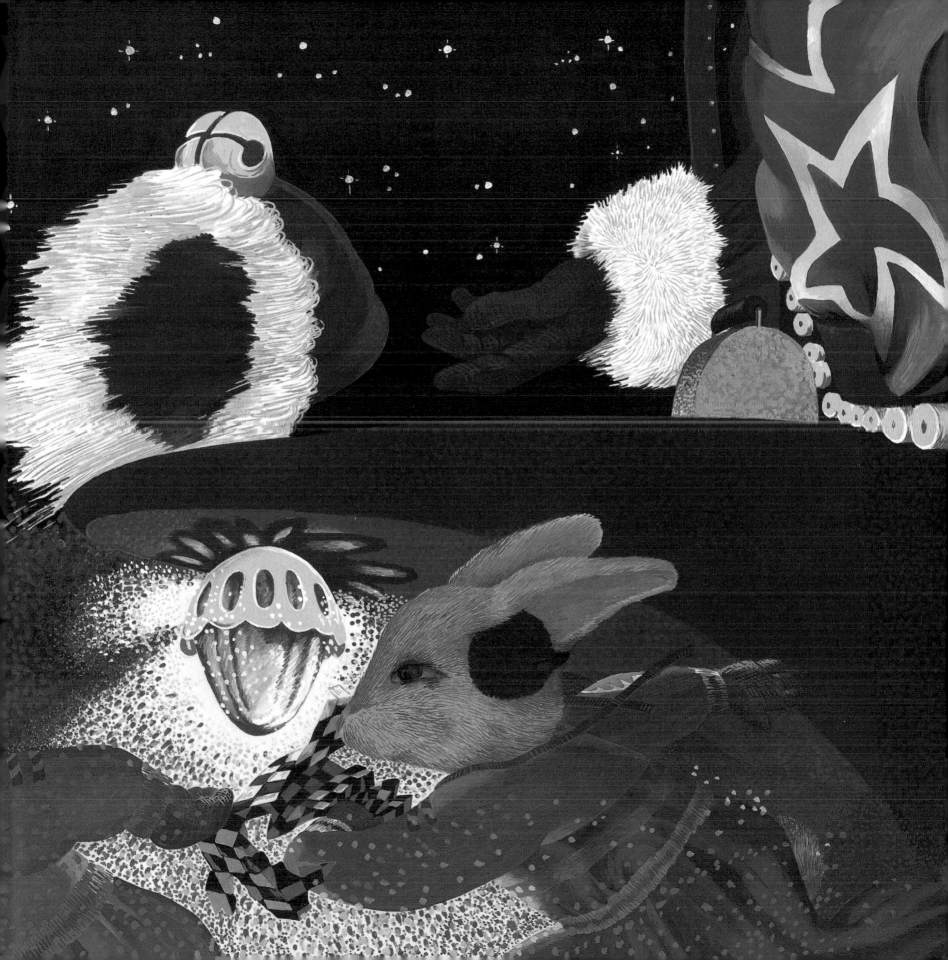

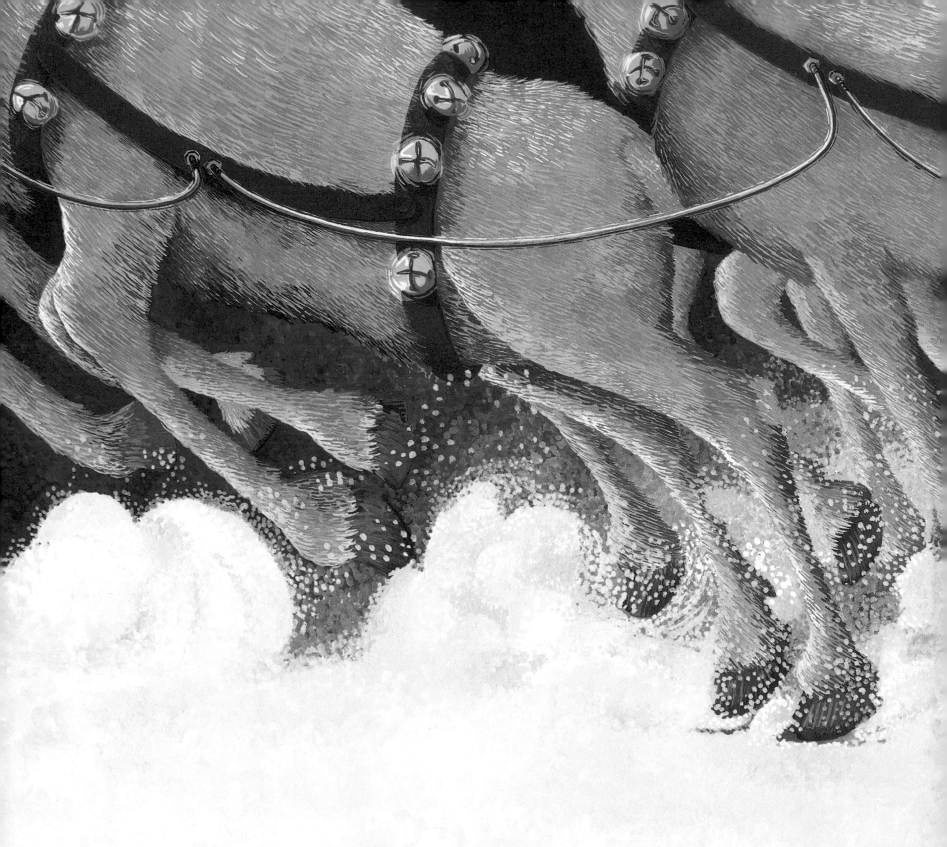

First a crunching of hooves on the snow,

Then the trembling of bells, and a jolly *"Let's go!"*

The moon casts a beam that touches the sleigh,
Then a whirlwind of stars lifts them up and away.

As the reindeer and sleigh rise into the glow,
Santa looks back. "Thank you, helpers! Ho, Ho!"

Gone!

Now our heartbeats are all we can hear.
No hooves, no sleigh bells, no cries of good cheer.

A shiver of snowy air tickles our skin.
It's time we were home in our beds, all tucked in.

While Santa is racing away toward the West,
His helpers can all get a good night's rest.

Shhh! Whisper Kringle O, Jingle O, Jolly Ho Ho.
We'll sleep with a secret that only we know.

All helpers are special in Santa's kind eyes,
So he rewards each with a special surprise.

Are you a helper? Then this much I can say:
You'll find *your* surprise on Christmas Day.